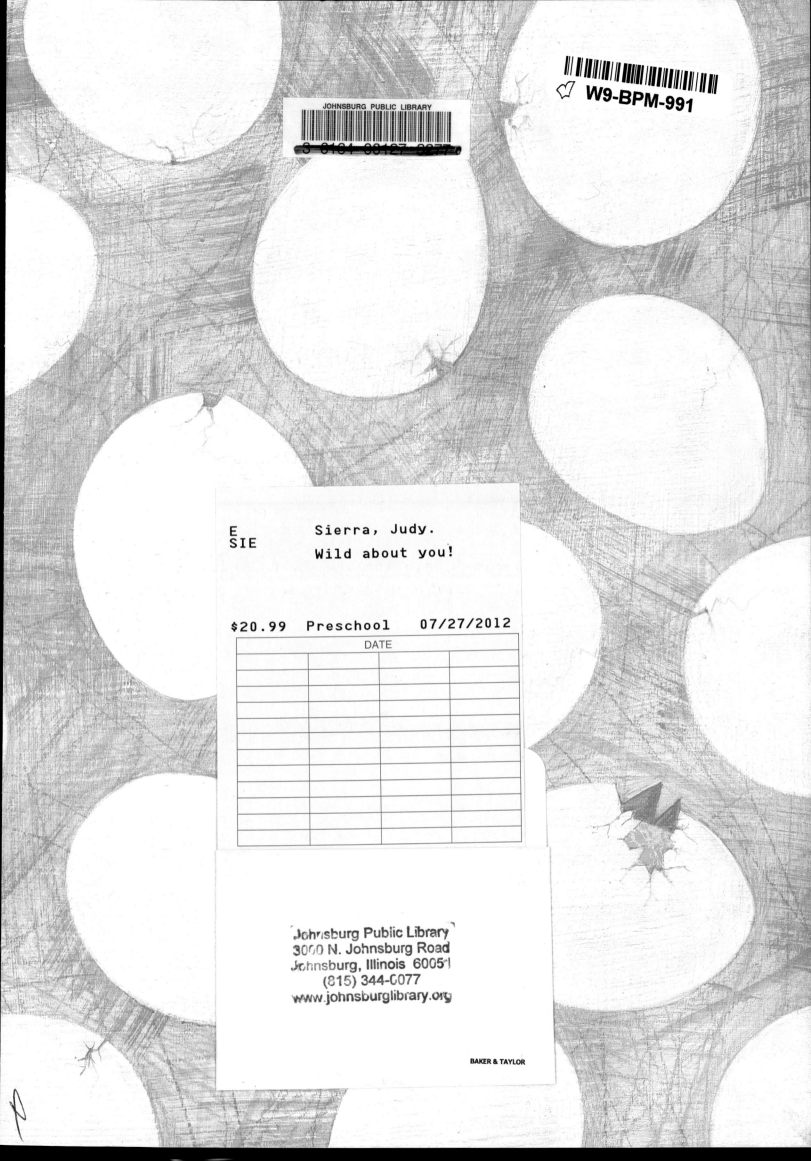

Wild About You!

Judy Sierra

pictures by

Marc Brown

Alfred A. Knopf ⟋ New York

Who's new at the zoo?

Brand-new babies, that's who!

Some popped from their mamas. Some hatched out of eggs.

Some walked right away on their long, wobbly legs.

Some babies are fluffy. Some babies are hairless.
Some babies are shy. Oops! Some are quite careless—
They wander away and get lost in the zoo.
And their mamas and papas can't find them. Can you?

"This just isn't fair," said the tree kangaroo.

"All my neighbors have babies—and *I want one, too!*"

"So do we," moaned the pandas. "WE'RE BLACK, WHITE, AND . . . BLUE."

"Blech! Babies are awful," the crocodiles told them.
"They bite and they scratch, and they howl when you hold them.
They won't do a thing that you want them to do.
And on top of all that, they make mountains of poo."

"May we have your babies?" the pandas asked sweetly.
"No! No!" cried their parents. "WE LOVE THEM COMPLETELY."

"G-r-r-r," grumbled the pandas. "It's *so-o-o* hard to wait."
Then a big orange van rumbled through the zoo gate.
And the sign on the van made their eyes open wide.
"Do you think there's a cub or a joey inside?"

They rushed to the van, and they peeked in the door.
On the floor lay a little brown box, nothing more.

"This egg is endangered," the zoo vet explained.

"Who would like to adopt it?"

"I can't," croaked the crane.

"It's too small," hissed the ostrich.

"It's too big!" squawked the auk.

"I haven't got space in my nest," screeched the hawk.

The tree kangaroo scrambled forward to snatch it.
She said, "I have room in my pouch. I will hatch it.
No matter what kind of a bird it might be,
It can live in my tree and sing sweetly to me."

She kept the egg cozy for week after week,
Till she heard the *tap-tap* of her new baby's beak.
"I've hatched out a penguin," she said. "Oh my word.
I wasn't expecting this sort of a bird."

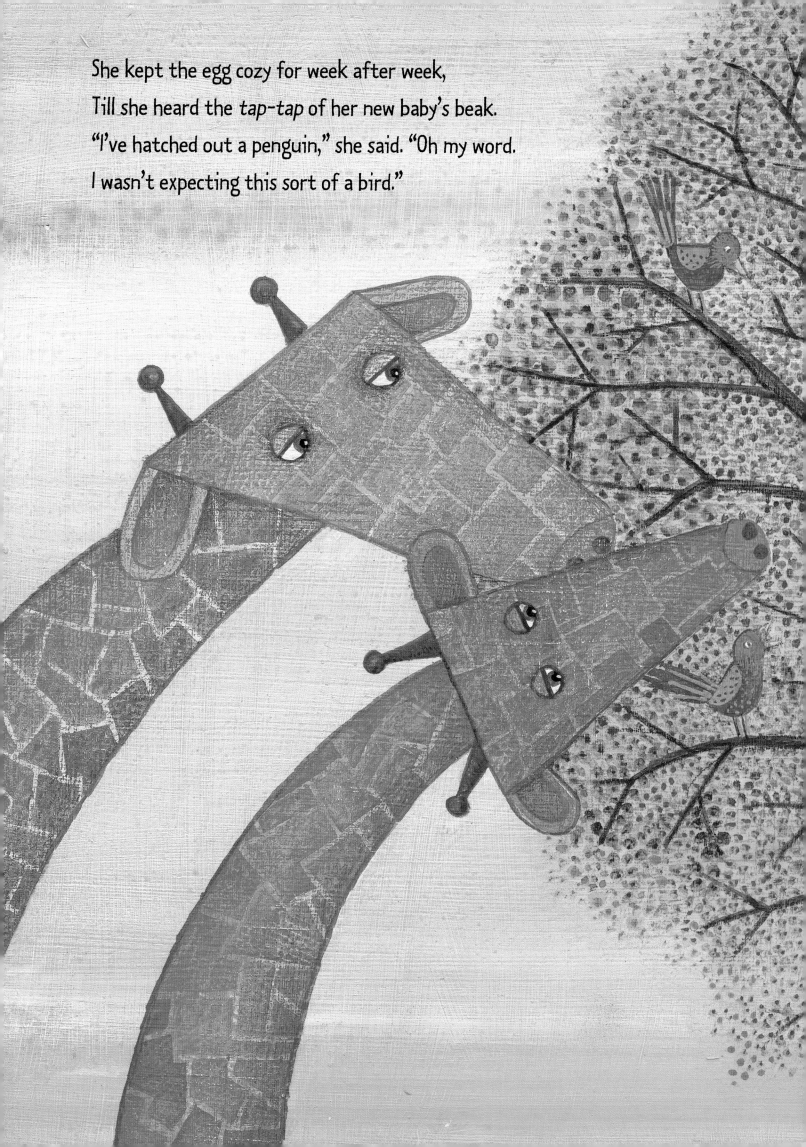

"Penguins don't fly. Penguins never sing sweetly.
But that doesn't matter. I LOVE YOU COMPLETELY!
Yes, you are the answer to all of my wishes.
Though I *may* need some help . . . because penguins eat fishes."

So the puffins delivered fresh fish every day.
The flamingos invited her over to play.
And one happy day, she hopped her first hop—
A super-sensational pengaroo bop.
Then she shouted, "Hey, Mom! I want back in my pouchy!"

The pandas, of course, were still gloomy and grouchy.

They rolled on the ground, groaning "Bah!" and "Boo-hoo!"

Then, beneath the bamboo, they heard someone say, *mew*.

And a kitten jumped onto Ms. Panda's wide lap,

Picked a comfortable spot, and curled up for a nap.

"What a curious cub," Mr. Panda declared.

"You're a kind of a sort of a cat of a bear.

You're roly. You're poly. You're quite pandalicous.

Yes, you are the answer to our wildest wishes."

The tigers stopped by with fresh milk every day.

The meerkats invited him over to play.

They snoozed in the shade of the kangaroo's tree.
And all were as happy as happy could be.

If you're looking for babies much newer than new,
Here's a cool pandacat! Here's a sweet pengaroo!
Every kid needs a family, we know that it's true.
And to bring up a baby . . .

IT TAKES A WHOLE ZOO!

For our incomparable editor, Janet Schulman

—J.S. & M.B.

THIS IS A BORZOI BOOK PUBLISHED BY ALFRED A. KNOPF

Text copyright © 2012 by Judy Sierra
Jacket art and interior illustrations copyright © 2012 by Marc Brown

All rights reserved. Published in the United States by Alfred A. Knopf, an imprint
of Random House Children's Books, a division of Random House, Inc., New York.

Knopf, Borzoi Books, and the colophon are registered trademarks of Random House, Inc.

Visit us on the Web! randomhouse.com/kids

Educators and librarians, for a variety of teaching tools,
visit us at randomhouse.com/teachers

Library of Congress Cataloging-in-Publication Data
Sierra, Judy.
Wild about you! / Judy Sierra.
p. cm.
Summary: Joining the new baby animals at the zoo are the much-loved pengaroo and the pandacat.
ISBN 978-0-307-93178-8 (trade) — ISBN 978-0-375-97107-5 (lib. bdg.)
[1. Stories in rhyme. 2. Zoo animals—Fiction. 3. Animals—Infancy—Fiction.] I. Title.
PZ8.3.S577Wi 2012
[E]—dc23
2011029010

The text of this book is set in 21-point Kosmik.
The illustrations were created using watercolor, gouache, and colored pencils on prepared wooden panels.

MANUFACTURED IN CHINA
August 2012
10 9 8 7 6 5 4 3 2 1

First Edition